I0889137

Walter Foster Jr.

learn to draw

Birds & Butterflies

Step-by-step instructions for more than 25 winged creatures

ILLUSTRATED BY ROBBIN CUDDY

This library edition published in 2016 by Walter Foster Jr.,
an imprint of Quarto Publishing Group USA Inc.
6 Orchard Road, Suite 100
Lake Forest, CA 92630

© 2016 Quarto Publishing Group USA Inc.
Published by Walter Foster Jr., an imprint of Quarto Publishing Group USA Inc.
All rights reserved. Walter Foster Jr. is trademarked.
Photographs © Shutterstock

Distributed in the United States and Canada by
Lerner Publisher Services
241 First Avenue North
Minneapolis, MN 55401 U.S.A.
www.lernerbooks.com

First Library Edition

Library of Congress Cataloging-in-Publication Data

Learn to draw birds & butterflies : step-by-step instructions for more than 25 animals / illustrated by Robbin Cuddy. -- First Library Edition.
pages cm
ISBN 978-1-939581-96-9
1. Birds in art--Juvenile literature. 2. Butterflies in art--Juvenile literature. 3. Drawing--Technique--Juvenile literature. I. Cuddy, Robbin, illustrator.
NC782.L43 2015
743.6'8--dc23

2015031438

9 8 7 6 5 4 3 2 1

MIX
Paper from responsible sources
FSC® C008080

Table of Contents

Tools & Materials

There's more than one way to bring birds and butterflies to life on paper—you can use crayons, markers, colored pencils, or even paints. Just be sure you have plenty of bright colors—yellows, oranges, blues, greens, and purples.

How to Use This Book

The drawings in this book are made up of basic shapes, such as circles, triangles, and rectangles. Practice drawing the shapes below.

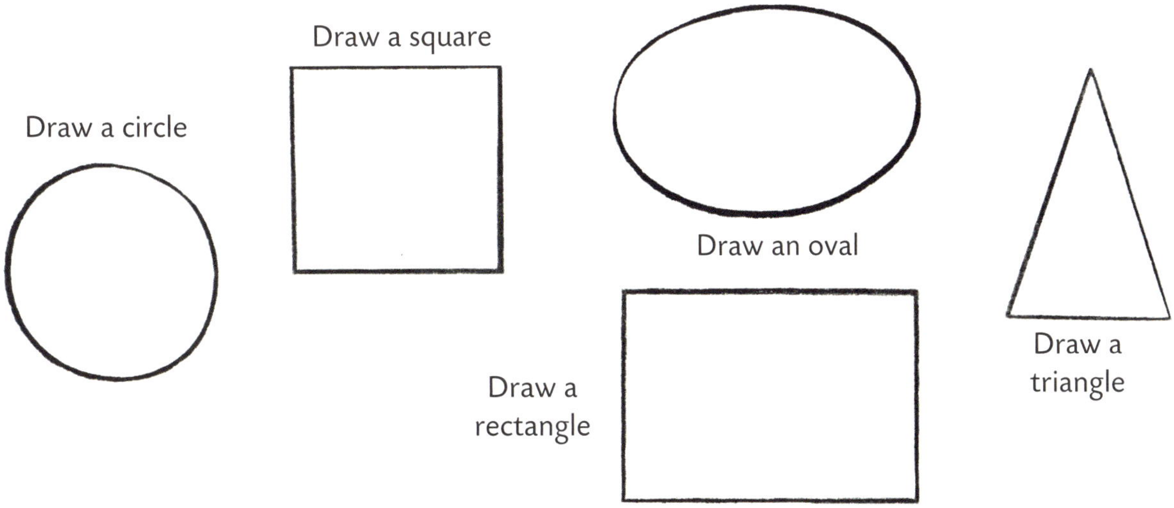

Notice how these drawings begin with basic shapes.

In this book, you'll learn about the size, diet, location, and appearance of each featured bird and butterfly. Look for mini quizzes along the way to learn new and interesting facts!

Look for this symbol, and check your answers on page 64!

Bird Basics

There are over 10,000 species of birds. They are feathered animals with wings and light bones (many of which are hollow), allowing most species to fly through the air. Many birds are also known for their pleasant chirps, calls, and whistles.

Birds fly by flapping their wings and using their tails to steer.

Birds rely on their excellent vision to gather information about their environment.

Did You Know?

Feathers are made of keratin, the same thing hair and nails are made of!

Bird Nesting

Birds do not give birth to live young; instead, they lay hard-shelled eggs in a nest. Because bird eggs are vulnerable to cold temperatures and predators, birds tend to them in their nests, keeping them warm and safe until they hatch.

Once the chicks break through their shells, the parents continue to help their babies by delivering food and even chewing it up for them!

Fun Fact!

Dinosaurs might look more like lizards, but birds are actually their closest relatives on Earth today!

Butterfly Basics

Butterflies are beautiful winged insects. They feed on the nectar of flowers along with some insects, such as aphids. Like bees, they help pollinate flowers.

Did You Know?

Butterflies can be found almost everywhere in the world!

The Life Cycle of a Butterfly

These insects are not born as butterflies; they hatch out of an egg as a caterpillar first!

1

An adult butterfly lays an egg.

2

The egg hatches into a caterpillar (or larva).

3

The caterpillar becomes a chrysalis (or pupa).

4

The chrysalis hatches into a butterfly.

5

The butterfly dries off its wings and flies away! The cycle repeats.

Fun Fact!

The life span of a butterfly varies depending on the species. Depending on the climate, most species stay caterpillars for two to three weeks before entering the chrysalis stage, which can last from a few days to many months. Once they hatch, most average adult butterflies live for about a month.

Northern Cardinal

Details

Size: 4.5 to 9.5 inches long
Diet: Seeds, nuts, fruits, and insects
Location: North America

Did You Know?

While the male cardinal has distinct red feathers and a black eye mask, the female cardinal has a paler, browner coloring. However, both males and females have sharp head crests and cone-shaped beaks that are great for opening nuts and seeds.

The northern cardinal is a songbird known for its beautiful whistle and bright red feathers. They live mainly in the southeastern parts of the United States.

Fun Fact!

The northern cardinal is the most popular state bird in the United States. Seven states have claimed this cardinal, including Illinois, Indiana, Kentucky, North Carolina, Ohio, Virginia, and West Virginia.

1

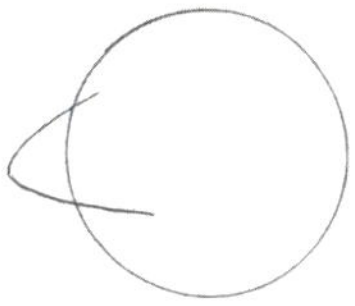

2

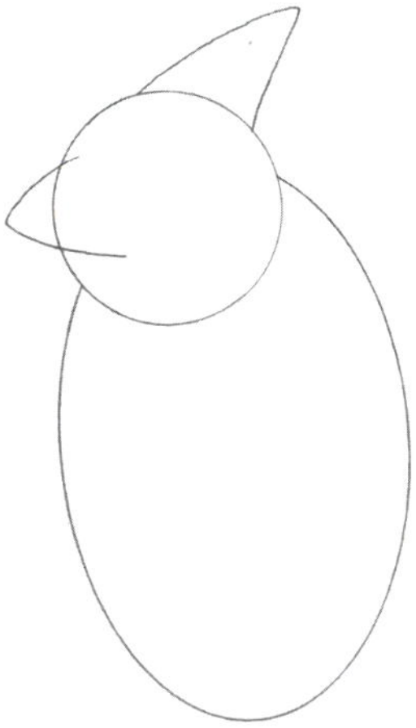

3

4

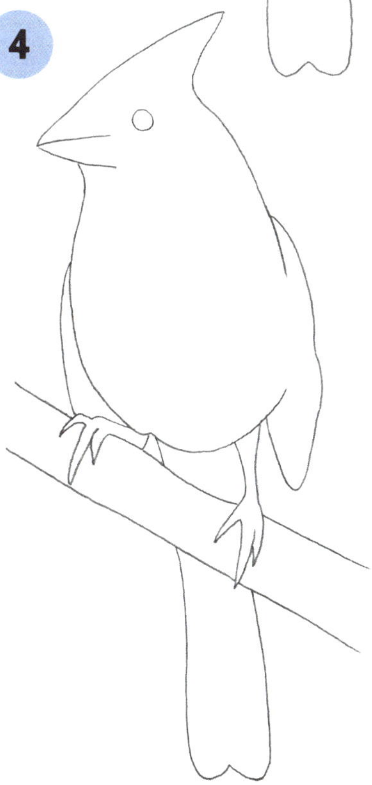

5

6

Green-Spotted Triangle

Details

Size: 2 to 3 inches
Diet: Nectar and fruit
Location: Australia and Indonesia

Did You Know?

The green-spotted triangle is known for its swift flying and fluttering. Like hummingbirds, they beat their wings rapidly while feeding at flowers.

Also called a Tailed Jay, this butterfly is brown or black with bright green spots. It has a small extension (or tail) on each hind wing.

1

2

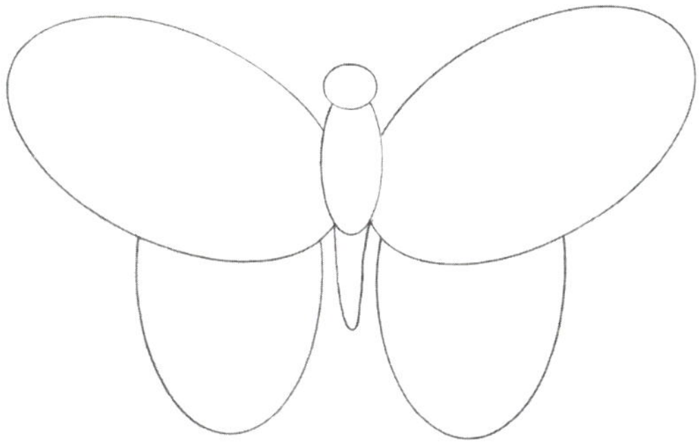

Mini Quiz

How long does it take for an egg to hatch and grow into an adult butterfly?

A. 1 week

B. 2 weeks

C. 5 weeks

D. 2 months

(Answer on page 64)

3

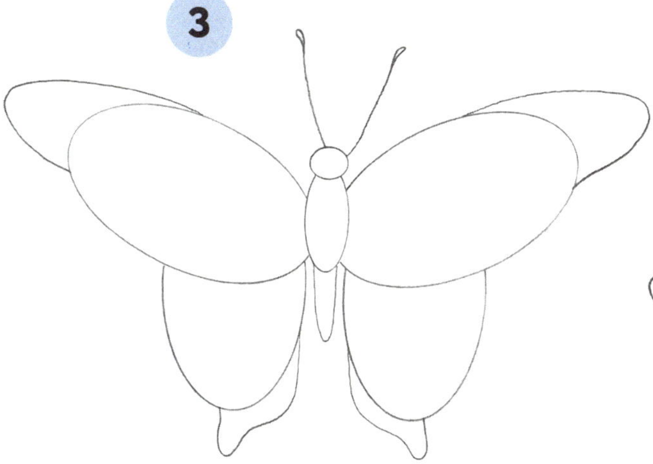

4

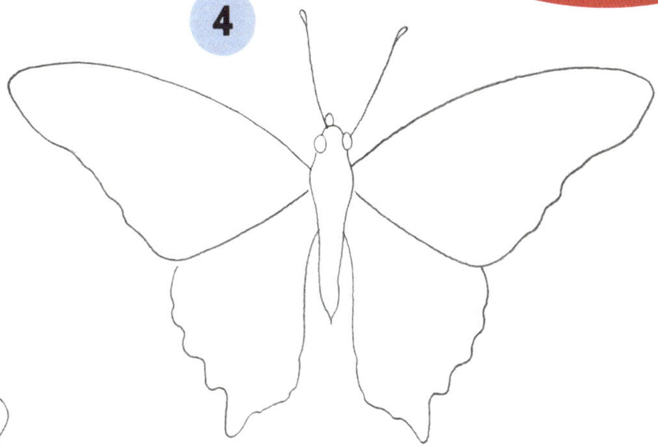

5

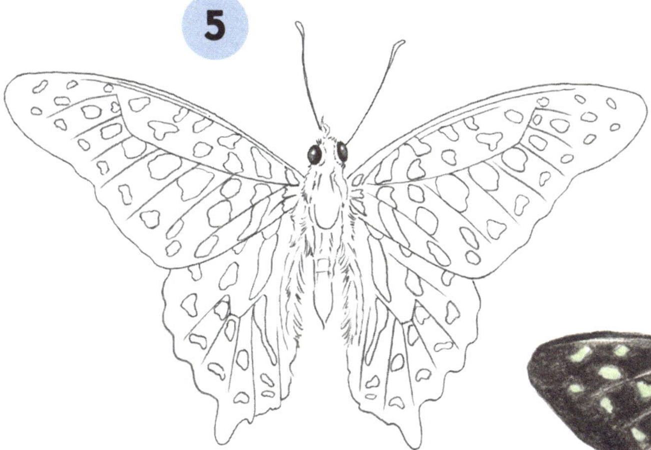

6

Flamingo

Did You Know?

The Spanish word for "flamingo" is *flamenco*, which relates the bird to its flame-like feathers. The word "flamenco" also refers to a Spanish dance.

The elegant flamingo is a long-legged bird with an S-shaped neck, a black-tipped beak, and a distinct plumage of pink feathers.

1

2

Fun Fact!

Flamingos are born with light gray feathers! A few years after birth, they turn pink as a result of their diet. The food they eat is rich in beta-carotene, which contains pigment that gives them an orangey-pink hue.

3

4

5

6

Peacock

Details

Size: 3 to 6 feet long
Diet: Seeds, grains, berries, insects, and worms
Location: India, Sri Lanka, Burma, Java, and Africa

Did You Know?

The word "peacock" refers only to the male birds, while "peahen" refers to the female birds. Because they need to blend into their environment while raising their young, peahens are generally less vibrant than peacocks and do not have long trains or grand feather displays.

The peacock is a male bird with a long tail train and a fan-like feather display. Colored with metallic blue, green, and bronze, each feather is tipped with an eyespot.

1

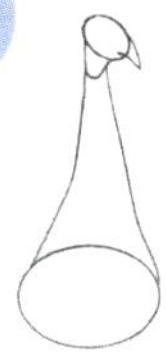

2

Fun Fact!

A peacock's train can reach 60 inches in length! To attract female mates, this bird lifts and spreads its tail feathers to form a beautiful fan, which it vibrates to create a shimmering effect.

3

5

4

6

Purple-Spotted Swallowtail

Fun Fact!

The scientific name of this butterfly is *Graphium weiskei*. These butterflies are known for gathering near moist sand or mud to drink mineral-rich water.

This beautifully colored butterfly features black wings with spots of purple, pink, blue, and green. It makes its home in high elevations of the rainforest.

Mini Quiz

True or False:
Like many species of butterfly, female purple spotted swallowtails look and behave differently than males.

(Answer on page 64)

1

2

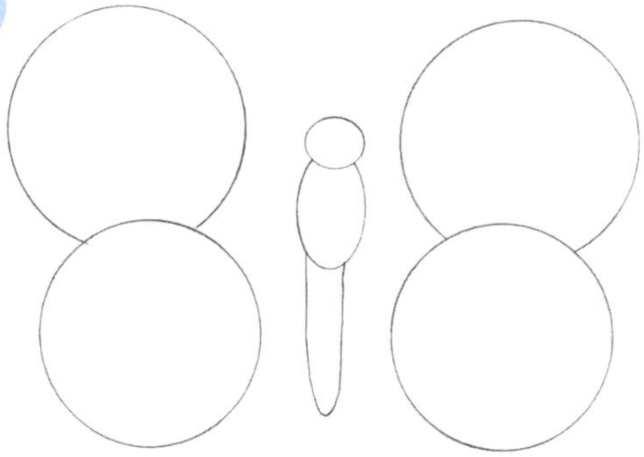

3

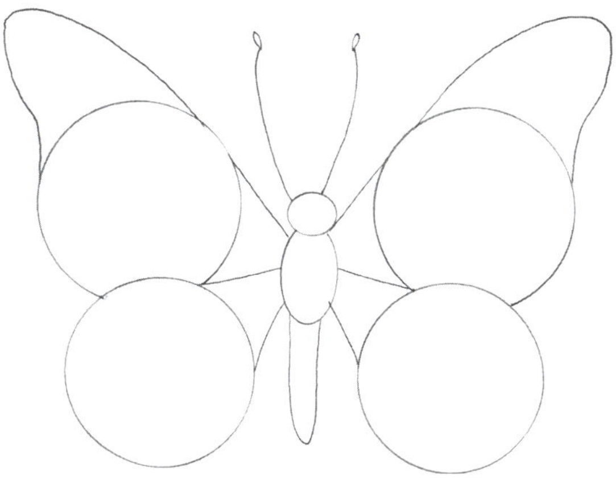

4

5

6

Blue Jay

Details

Size: 12 inches long
Diet: Seeds, nuts, small creatures, and eggs
Location: Eastern and central areas of North America

Did You Know?

Blue jays are social birds with tight family relationships. They are very vocal and protective of their nests. once they lay their eggs, it takes about 16 to 20 days for them to hatch!

This bird has a pointed head crest, a black beak, and brilliant feathers of blue, white, and black. These noisy birds inhabit the forests of North America.

1

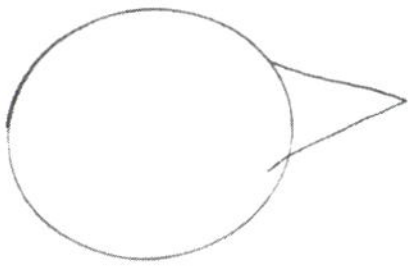

2

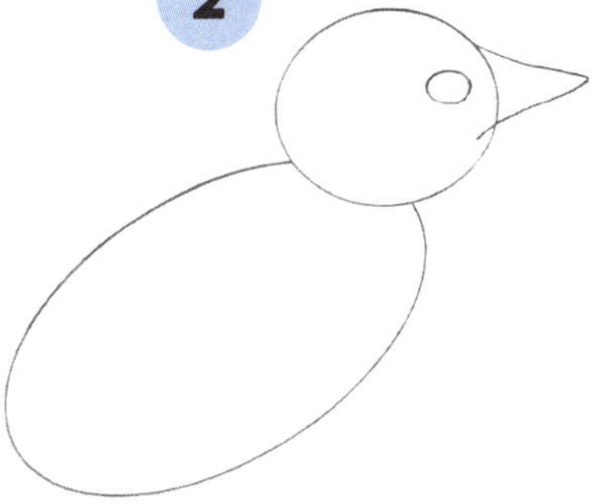

Mini Quiz

Which city uses the blue jay as the mascot for its professional baseball team?

A. Chicago
B. New York
C. Washington, D.C.
D. Toronto

(Answer on page 64)

3

4

5

6

Adonis Blue

Details

Size: 1.5 inches
Diet: Nectar
Location: Europe and the United Kingdom

Did You Know?

The bright blue of this butterfly covers only the upper side of its wings. The underside, visible when the butterfly is perched with its wings up, is a brownish-gray with black spots and orange markings.

Males of the Adonis blue butterfly species are brilliant blue in color with white and black edges. They prefer the warm areas of Europe and the Middle East.

Mini Quiz

What color is the Adonis blue female?

A. Blue
B. Brown
C. Black
D. White

(Answer on page 64)

1

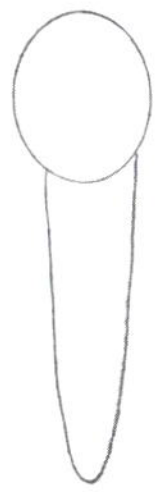

2

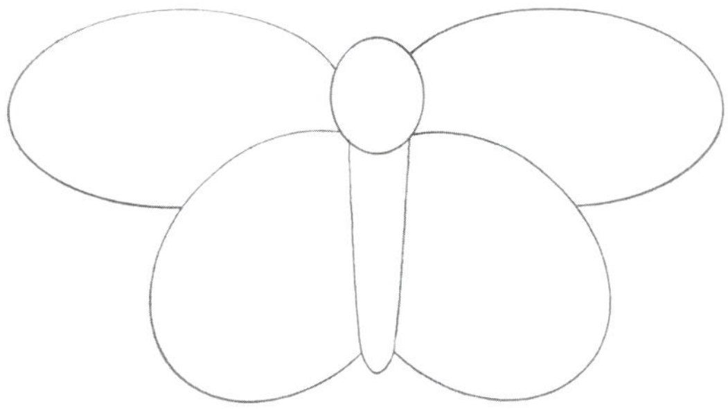

3

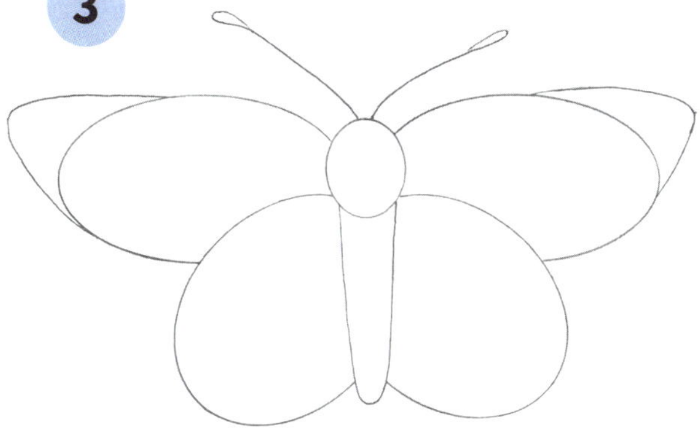

4

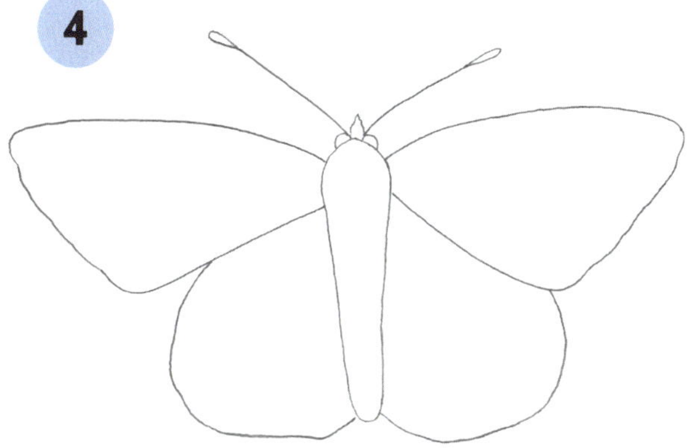

5

6

Toucan

Size: Up to 24 inches long

Diet: Fruit, lizards, bird eggs, and insects

Location: Central and South America

Did You Know?

The toucan is known for its large, curved beak, which is about one-third the size of its body. Made of keratin, this brightly colored tool helps the toucan access food. Some scientists think it also serves to intimidate predators.

Toucans are loud, large-billed birds from Central and South America. Most have black-feathered bodies with white or yellow necks and colorful beaks.

Fun Fact!

Known for being the loudest of the forest birds, these tropical treetop dwellers live and travel in flocks.

1

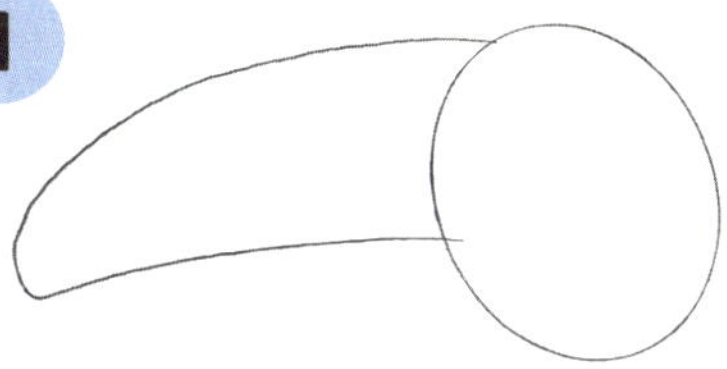

2

3

4

5

6

Red-Banded Hairstreak

Location: Southeastern United States

Size: 1 inch

Diet: Nectar

Fun Fact!

The red-banded hairstreak has small tails and eyespots that create the illusion of a head on its backside. This feature protects its actual head from being attacked by predatory spiders.

This gray butterfly has a red streak along with fine black and white lines on the underside of each wing. Its legs and antennae are covered in black and white bands.

1

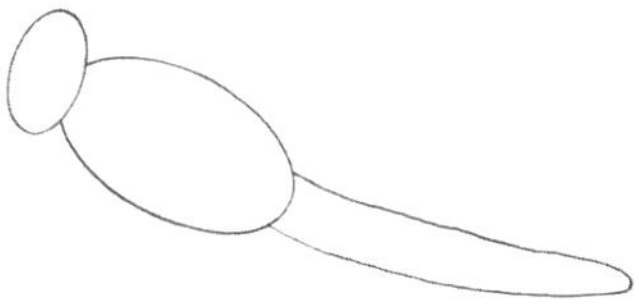

2

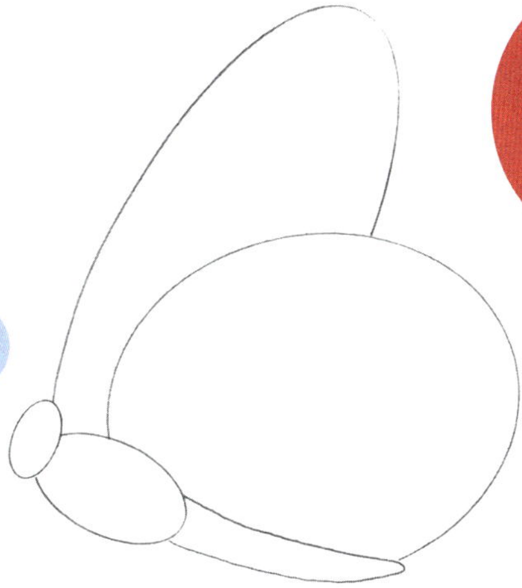

Mini Quiz

Which type of leaf is the favorite food of the red-banded hair-streak caterpillar?

A. Sumac
B. Stinging nettle
C. Milkweed
D. Oak

(Answer on page 64)

3

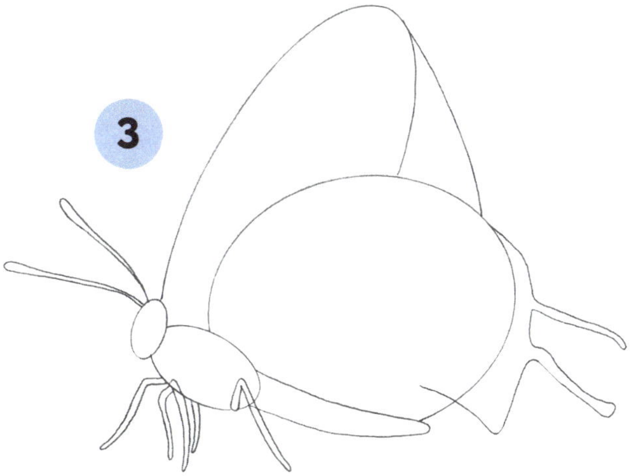

4

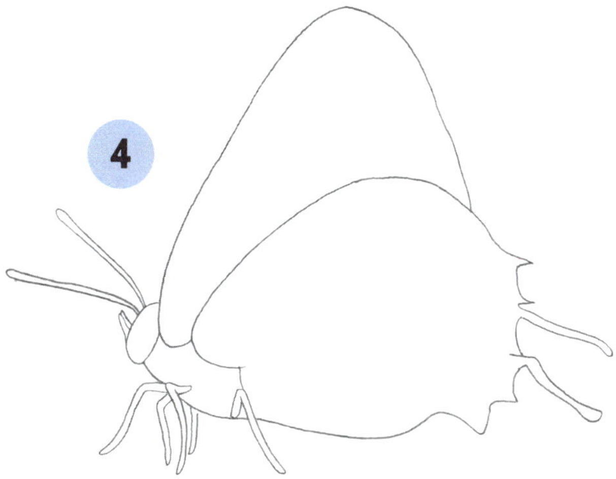

5

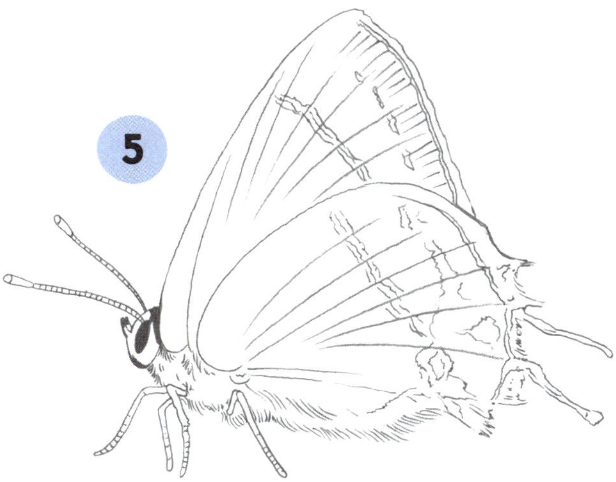

6

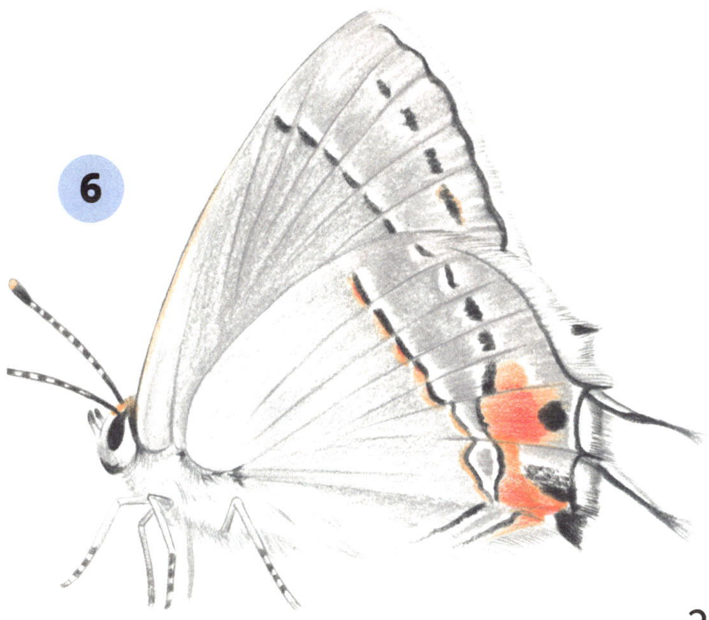

Baltimore Oriole

Details

Size: 8.5 inches long
Diet: Insects, caterpillars, fruit, and nectar
Location: North America

Did You Know?

Orioles are known for their excellent nest-building skills. Using twigs, grasses, hair, and other found materials, the female oriole builds a nest that hangs from the end of a tree branch. The male defends the nest from predators while the female tends to the eggs or chicks.

As the official state bird of Maryland, the Baltimore Oriole has a black head; black wings with a white bar on each; and a bright orange underside.

Mini Quiz

The Baltimore Oriole is the official mascot for which professional sport in Maryland?

A. Football
B. Baseball
C. Basketball
D. Hockey

(Answer on page 64)

1

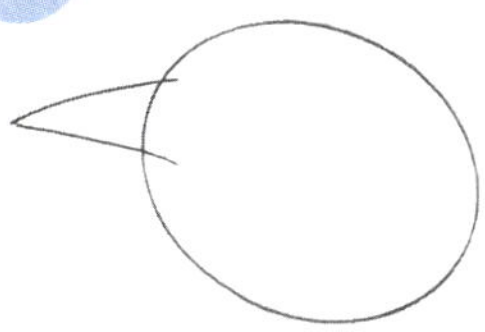

2

3

4

5

6

Red Admiral

Details

Size: 3 inches
Diet: Rotting fruit, sap, and nectar
Location: North and Central America, Europe, Asia, New Zealand, and North Africa

Did You Know?

Stinging nettle is the host plant for red admiral caterpillars. But remember: Don't touch stinging nettle without gloves! This herbaceous plant is protected by stinging hairs on its stems and the undersides of its leaves.

The red admiral is a brownish-black butterfly with red-orange bands and scalloped wings. This migratory species is one of the most widespread butterflies on earth!

1

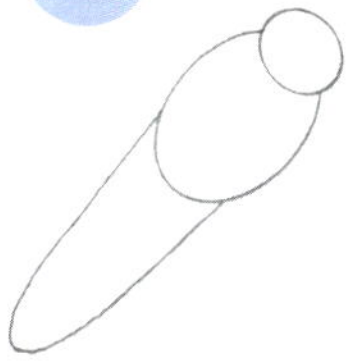

2

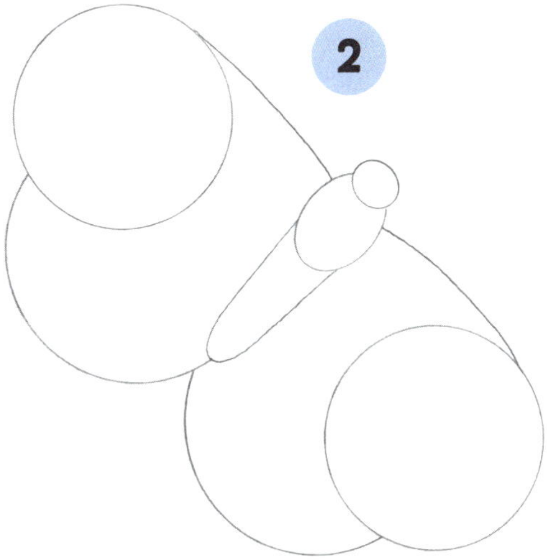

Fun Fact!

The red admiral is bold and curious. If you ever see one in your garden, it may very well land on you!

3

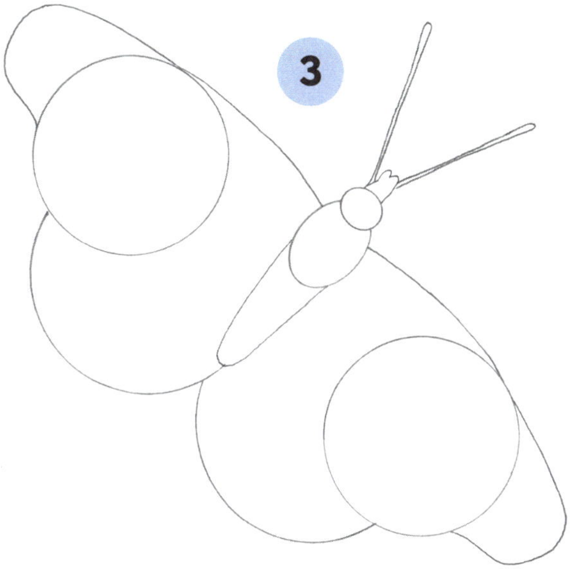

4

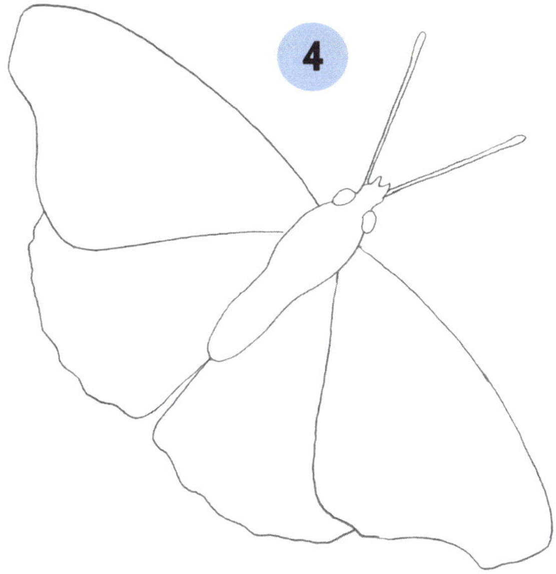

5

6

Cedar Waxwing

Did You Know?

The word "waxwing" refers to the tips of this bird's wings, which are coated in a shiny red material. Scientists still do not know the purpose of this wax-like feature!

The cedar waxwing is a fruit-eating bird with a flat crest, yellow underside, black eye mask, and boxy yellow- or orange-tipped tail.

1

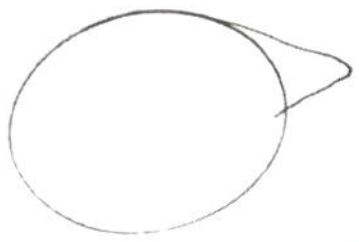

2

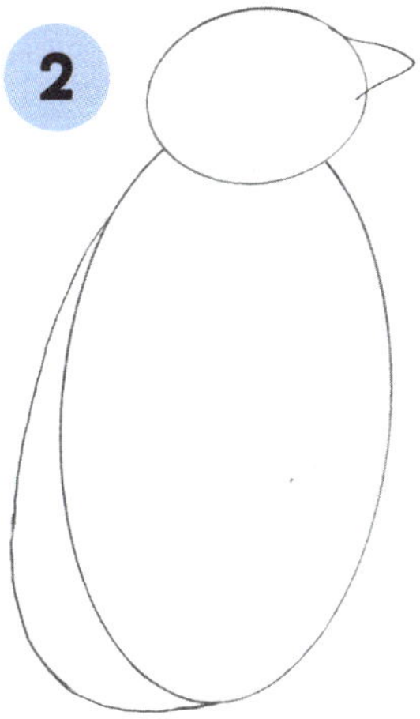

3

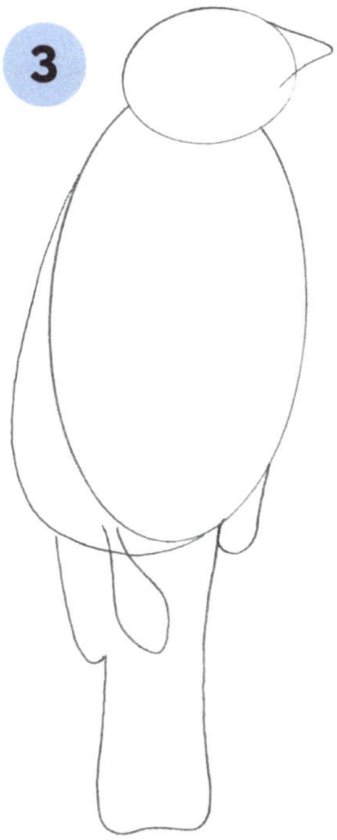

Mini Quiz

What is the cedar waxwing's primary source of food?

A. Worms

B. Grains

C. Grapes

D. Berries

(Answer on page 64)

4

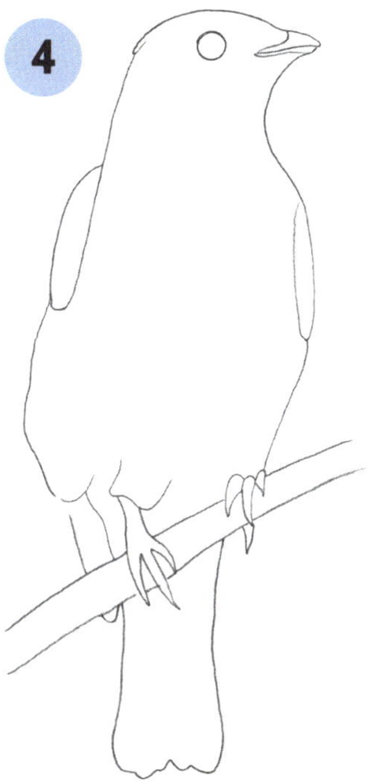

5

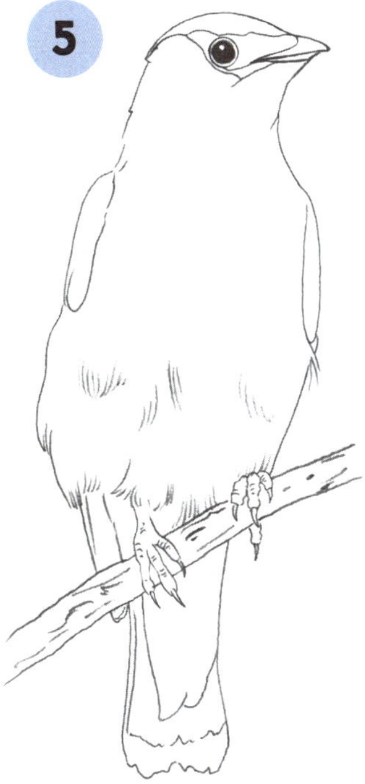

6

Peacock Butterfly

Details

Size: 2 inches
Diet: Nectar, sap, and fruit
Location: Europe and Asia

Did You Know?

An eyespot is a part of an animal's coloring that tricks predators into believing it's the eye of a different animal. The eyespots of the peacock butterfly are an effective defense against bird predators!

The peacock butterfly has reddish wings and purple eyespots. It is a very common butterfly in Europe, spotted often in gardens, parks, and fields.

Fun Fact!

The underside of the peacock butterfly is made up of neutral grays and browns, with lines that mimic leaf veins. When perched with its wings up, the peacock's leaf-like appearance makes it difficult for predators to spot!

1

2

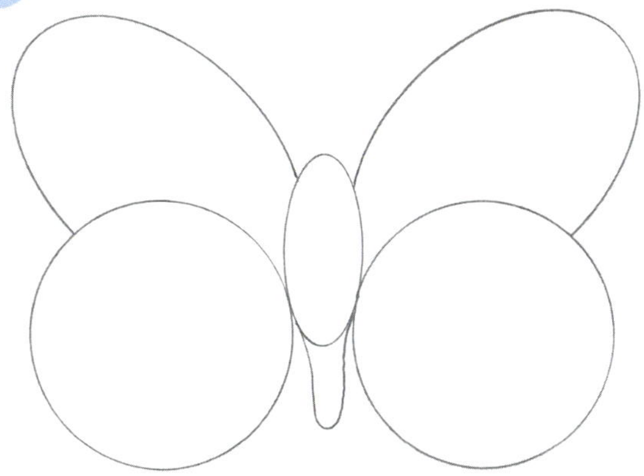

3

4

5

6

American Goldfinch

Did You Know?

The American goldfinch is sometimes called the "wild canary" or the "eastern goldfinch."

This sprightly, meadow-dwelling bird has feathers that range from bright yellow to brown. It has a small, sharp beak and black markings on the head, wings, and tail.

1

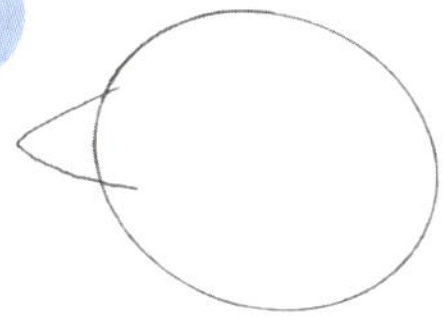

2

3

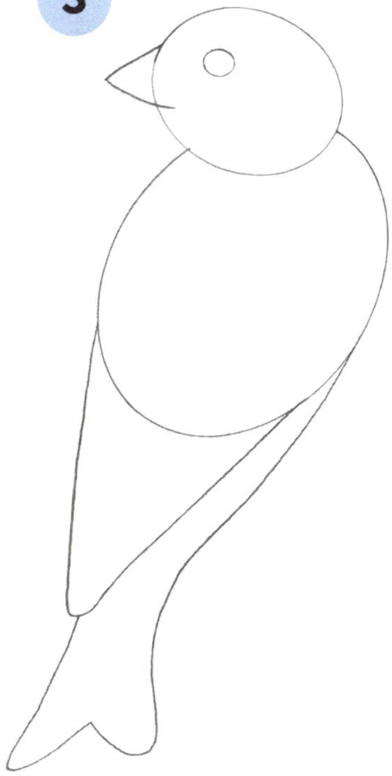

Fun Fact!

The goldfinch changes colors depending on the season. In summer, males have bright yellow feathers. In winter, they change to a light brown color, which helps them blend into a duller, snowier environment.

4

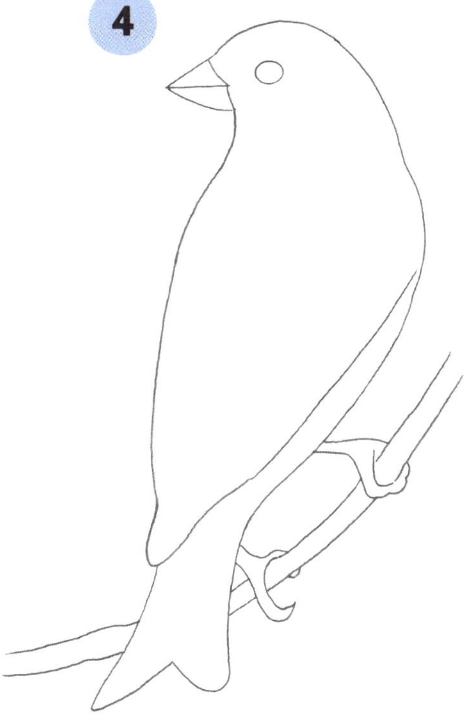

5

6

Monarch

Did You Know?

Around the start of autumn, monarch butterflies gather in large groups and migrate south to Mexico for the winter. When spring arrives in March, the monarchs fly north.

The monarch butterfly is known for its bright orange, black, and white coloring. It is the only butterfly that makes a two-way migration based on the seasons.

Fun Fact!

The easy-to-spot monarch butterfly does not need to blend into its environment. Its bright appearance warns predators that it is poisonous and unpleasant in taste!

1

2

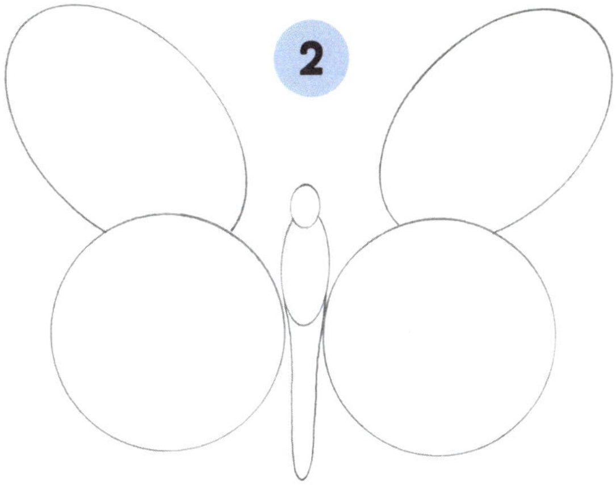

3

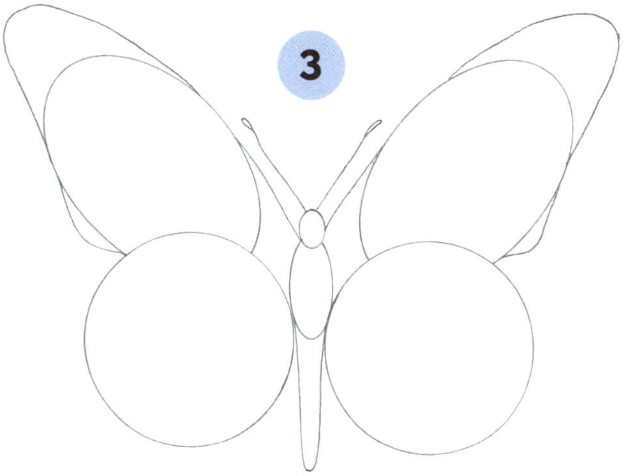

4

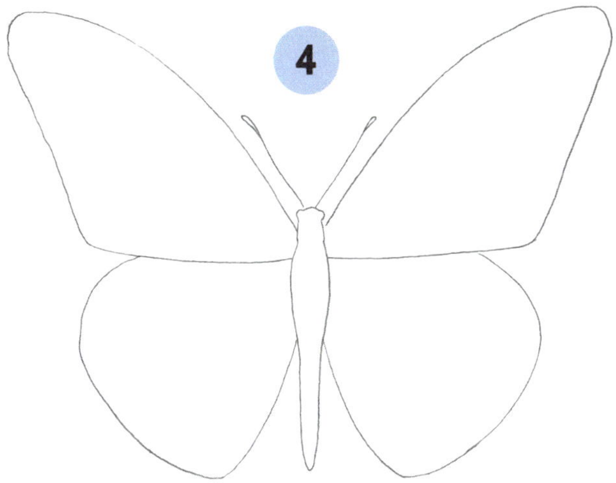

5

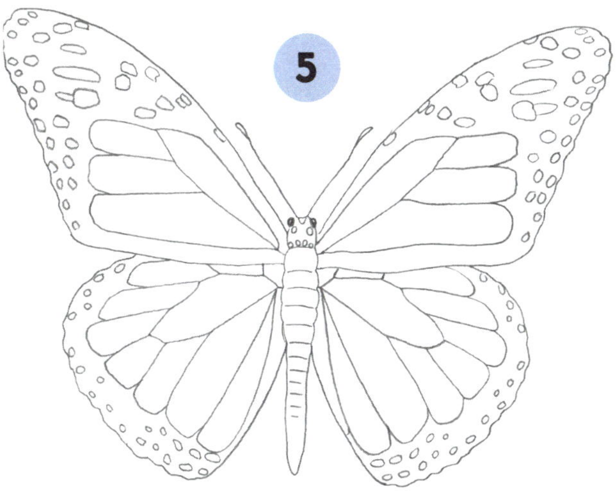

6

Gouldian Finch

Details

Size: 5 inches long
Diet: Seeds, fruit, insects, worms, and other small animals
Location: Australia

Did You Know?

Male Gouldian finches are usually brighter than females. An easy way to tell the difference between a male and female is to look at the chest: a male's chest is usually bright purple, whereas a female's is a softer mauve.

Also called the "rainbow finch," this Australian bird is known for its colorful plumage, which often includes red, black, gold, purple, green, blue, white, and silver.

1

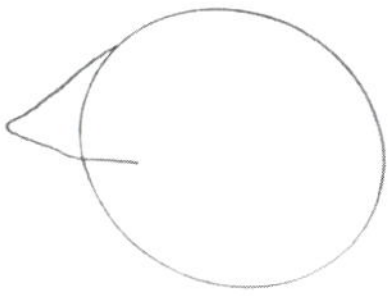

2

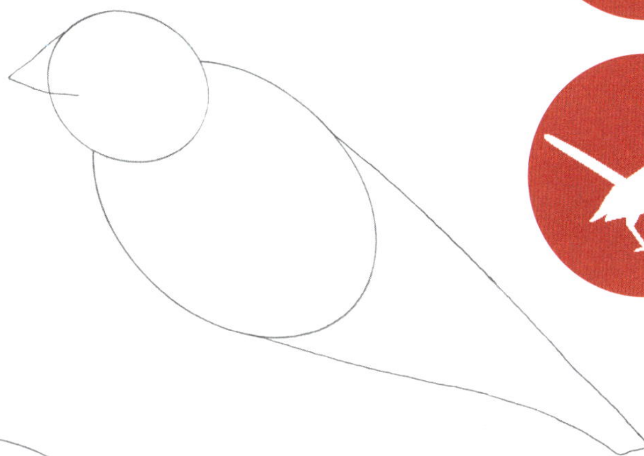

Mini Quiz

What does the term "molting" mean?

A. The process of shedding feathers
B. The process of building a nest
C. The process of migrating
D. The process of grooming

(Answer on page 64)

3

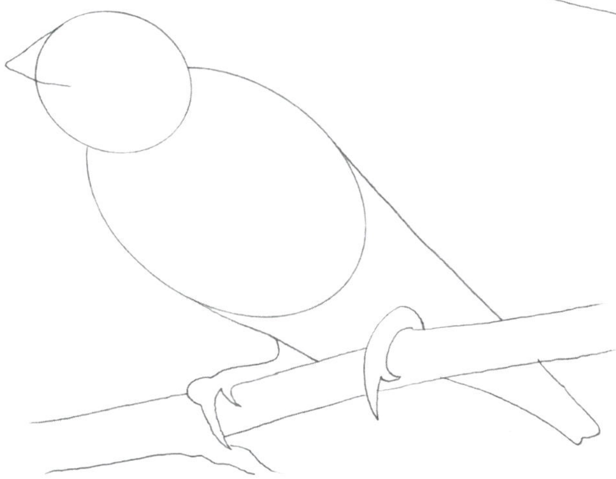

4

5

6

Redspot Sawtooth

Details

Size: 1.25 inches
Diet: Nectar
Location: Asia

Did You Know?

The redspot sawtooth has an evil twin! It looks very similar to a poisonous butterfly called the painted jezebel, which also lives in Asia.

This striking butterfly has black edges and veins, white forewings, and white and yellow hind wings with a red spot near the body.

1

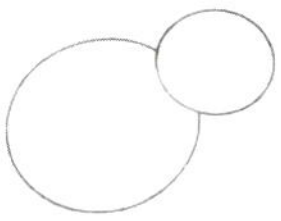

2

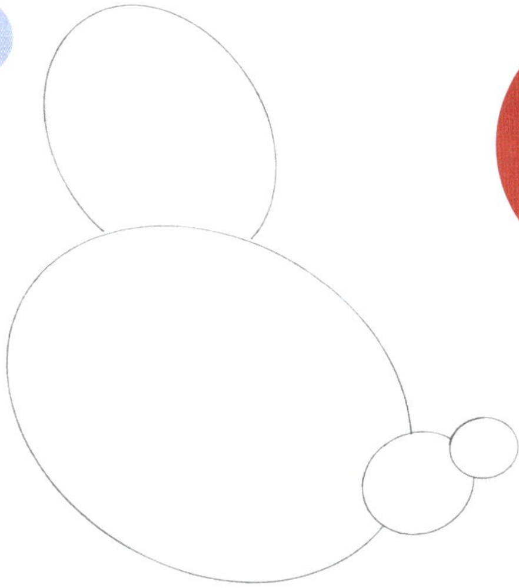

Mini Quiz

Which of the following describes the redspot sawtooth?

A. Tiny

B. Slow

C. Fast

D. Deadly

(Answer on page 64)

3

4

5

6

Scarlet Macaw

Details

Size: 32 inches long
Diet: Seeds, nuts, berries, and fruit
Location: Central and South America

Did You Know?

From squawks and screams to whistles and squeals, scarlet macaws are noisy birds! They can also imitate the human voice; as pets, they can learn several words and phrases.

The scarlet macaw looks like a traditional parrot—red, blue, and yellow with a naked eye mask and a sharp, curved beak.

1

2

3

Fun Fact!

The scarlet macaw can live up to 80 years in captivity! In the wild, it generally lives between 30 and 50 years.

4

5

6

Large Orange Tip

Details

Size:
1.5 to 2 inches
Diet: Nectar
Location: Europe

Did You Know?

Host plants for these caterpillars include lady's-smock and garlic mustard.

The males of this species have white wings tipped with bright orange. They can be seen flying in damp habitats during the months of April and May.

1

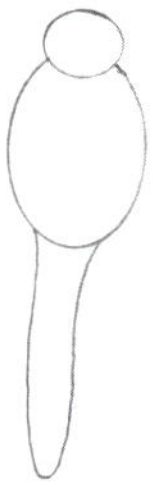

2

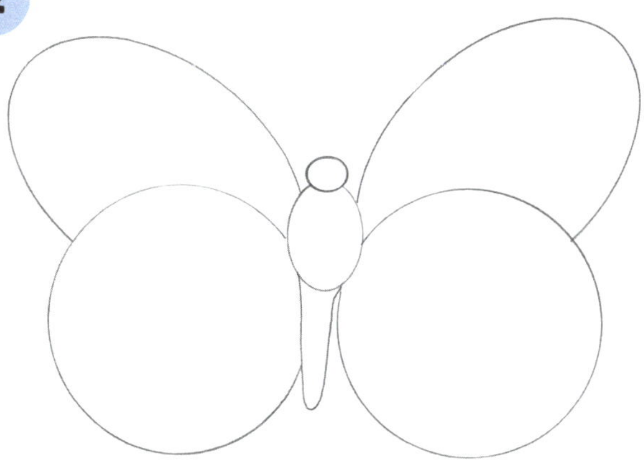

Mini Quiz

What color is the female butterfly of this species?

A. Orange
B. White
C. Black
D. Brown

(Answer on page 64)

3

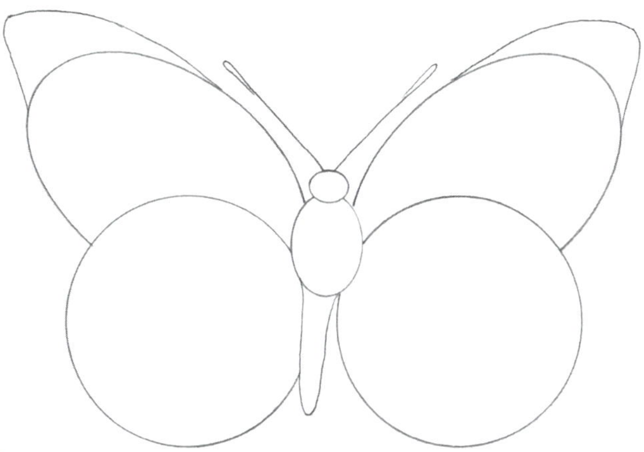

4

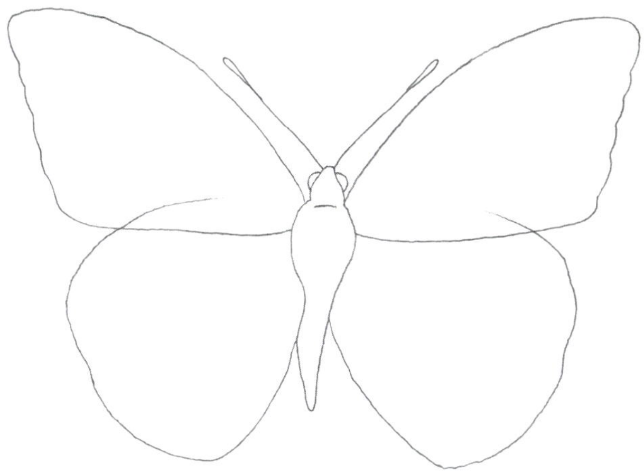

5

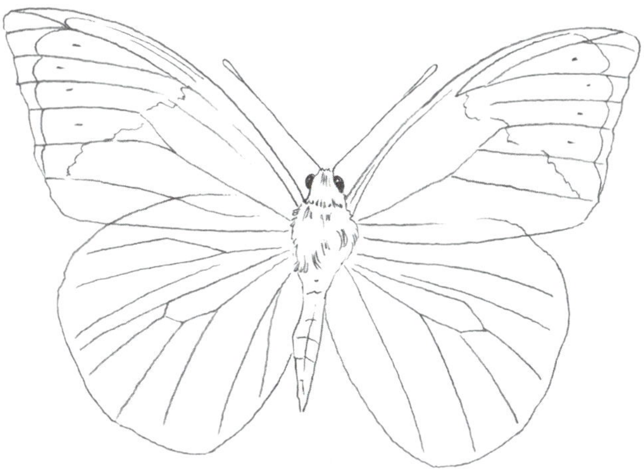

6

Kingfisher

Did You Know?

The kingfisher's long, sharp beak helps it hunt for prey; as it flies over still water, it will pluck out or even spear a fish with its beak. Sometimes it uses its beak to dig for prey in the mud.

The kingfisher has a pointed beak and blue or teal feathers with an orange underside. They live and feed near lakes, rivers, streams, and coastlines.

1

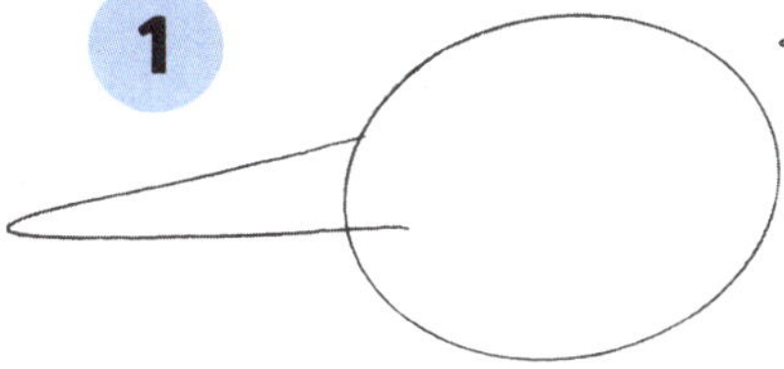

2

Mini Quiz

True or False:
The kingfisher makes its nest in trees near the water.

(Answer on page 64)

3

4

5

6

Common Blue

Details

Size: 1.25 inches
Diet: Nectar
Location: Europe, Asia, and North Africa

Did You Know?

Host plants for this caterpillar include bird's foot, black medick, and white clover.

The upper side of the male common blue butterfly is a blue-violet color with white edging. The underside is a brownish gray spotted with black and orange.

Fun Fact!

They don't call it "common" for nothing! The common blue butterfly is the most widespread butterfly in Britain.

1

2

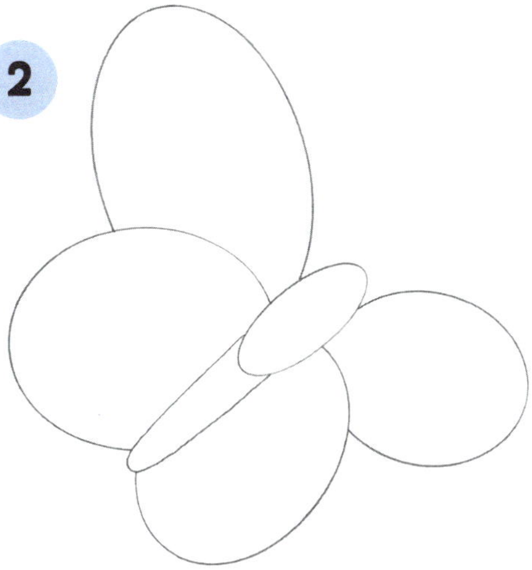

3

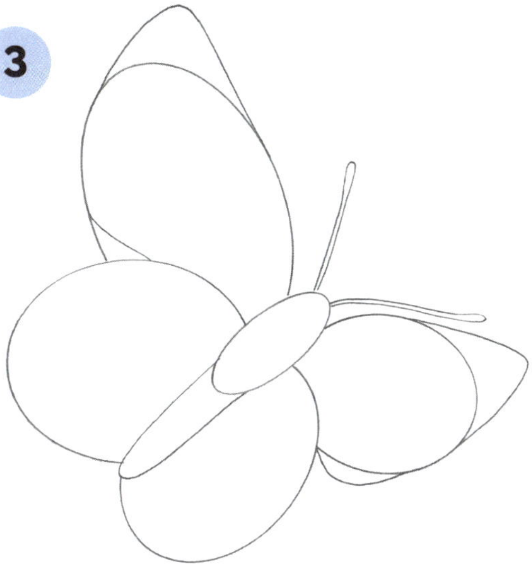

4

5

6

Ruby-Throated Hummingbird

Details

Size: 3 to 4 inches long
Diet: Nectar and insects
Location: North and Central America

Did You Know?

During cold nights, the ruby-throated hummingbird experiences periods of sleep or inactivity called "torpor." In this state, the bird's heart rate and body temperature drop to help it conserve energy.

This bird has iridescent feathers and a patch of red over its throat. It also has a long, thin beak designed to collect nectar from flowers.

Fun Fact!

The ruby-throated hummingbird beats its wings about 50 times per second!

1

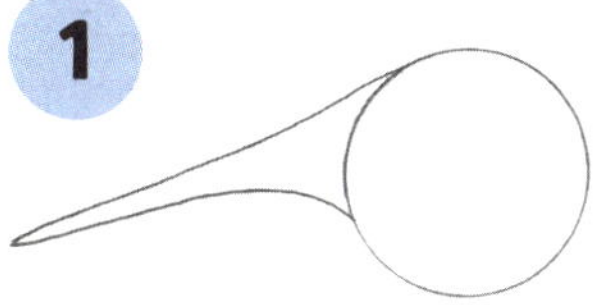

2

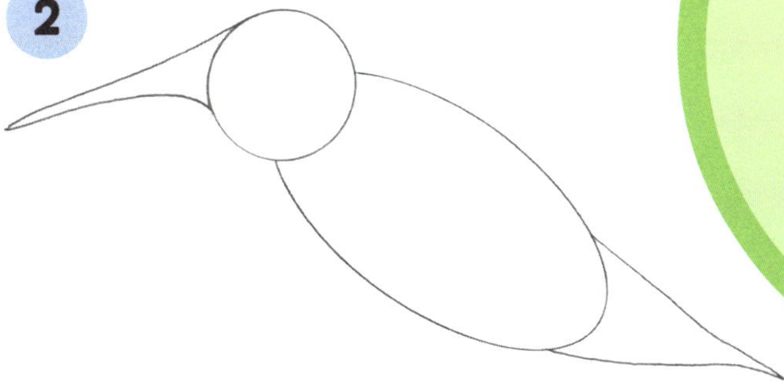

3

4

5

6

Ladder-Backed Woodpecker

Location: North and Central America

Diet: Insects, berries, and fruit

Size: 7 inches long

Did You Know?

Also known as the "cactus woodpecker," this bird prefers dry desert environments. It even makes its nests in cactus plants!

This striking bird has a red cap and a sharp, black bill. In a resting position, the ladder-backed woodpecker has black and white stripes across its back.

1

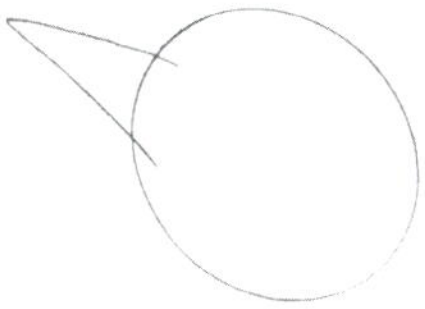

2

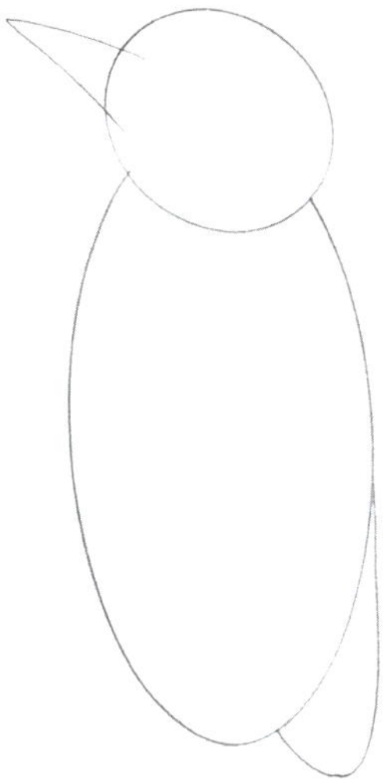

Mini Quiz

In which state is the ladder-backed woodpecker NOT found?

A. California
B. Texas
C. Arizona
D. Florida

(Answer on page 64)

3

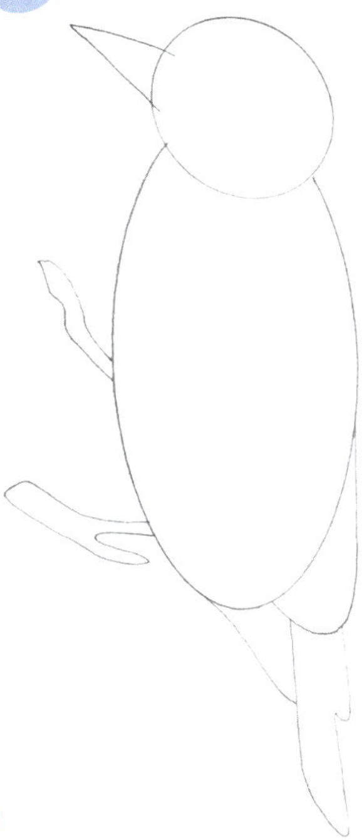

4

5

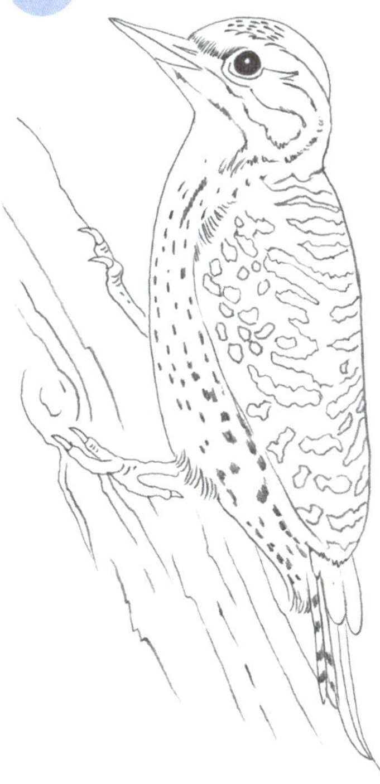

6

Black-Veined White

Did You Know?

Host plants for these caterpillars include hawthorns and rose plants, along with apple and cherry trees.

This butterfly has nearly transparent wings with black or brown veins. It prefers living and feeding along forest edges.

1

2

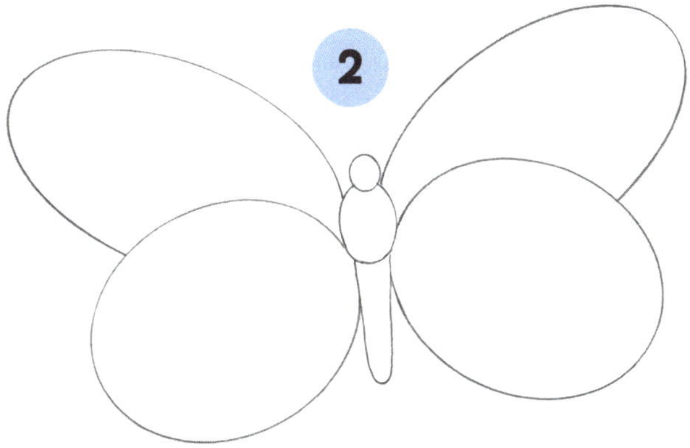

Mini Quiz

True or False:
The black-veined white butterfly can no longer be found in Britain.

(Answer on page 64)

3

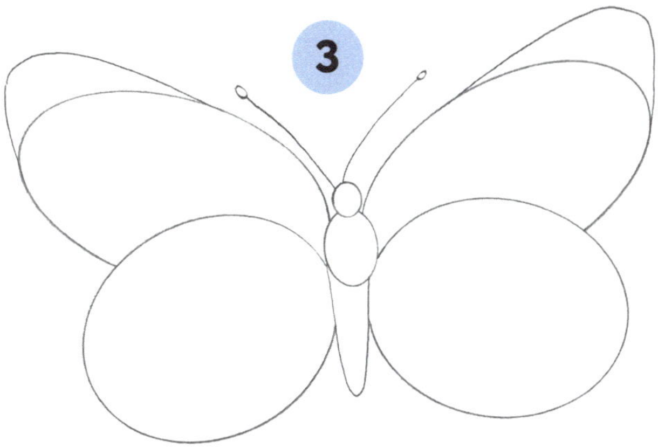

4

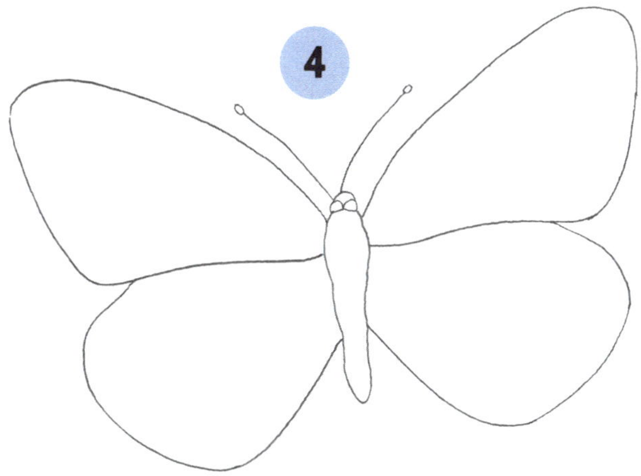

5

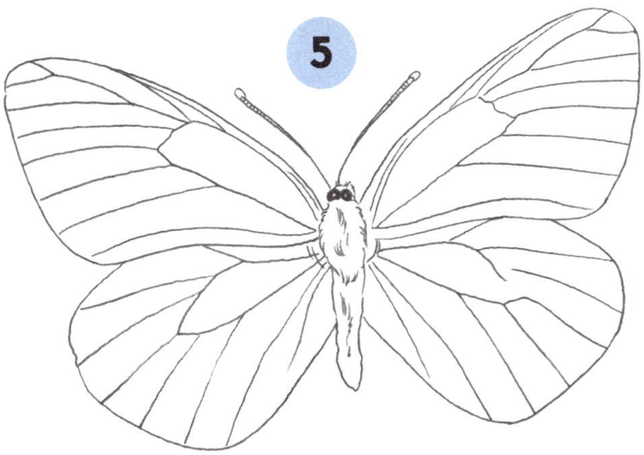

6

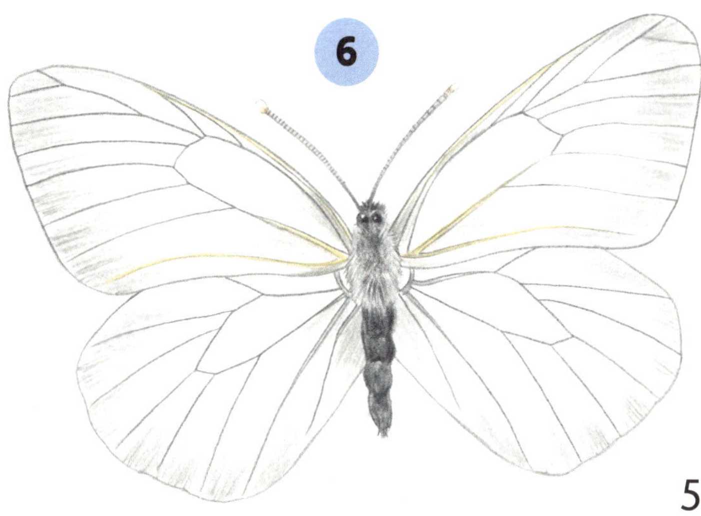

Pearl-Spotted Owlet

Did You Know?

Unlike many other species of owl, the pearl-spotted owlet does not have any ear tufts. Instead, it has a pair of ear holes buried beneath its feathers.

This small owl has white and brown feathers, yellow eyes, and a long tail. Its whistled calls can be heard in the savannahs and scrub forests of Southern Africa.

Fun Fact!

Many believe that all owls are nocturnal, a term for animals that are most active at night. However, the pearl-spotted owlet is the most diurnal (or day-active) owl in Southern Africa.

1

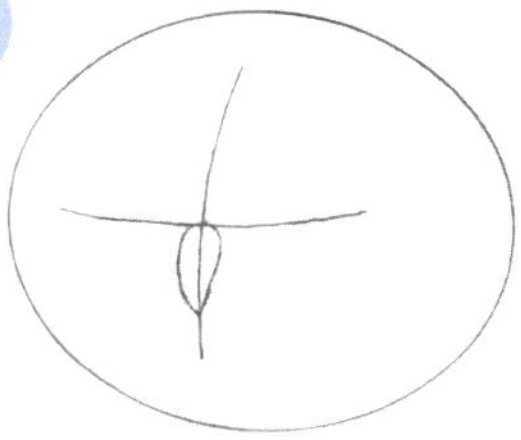

2

3

4

5

6

Common Birdwing

Did You Know?

The host plant of the common birdwing is called Indian birthwort or Dutchman's pipe—a vine plant with purple flowers.

The common birdwing is a striking Asian butterfly with black forewings and bright yellow, black-spotted hind wings. It has a yellow abdomen and a crimson neck.

Fun Fact!

Birdwing butterflies are some of the largest butterflies in the world. The Queen Alexandra's birdwing (of Papua New Guinea) has a wingspan of about 10 inches!

1

2

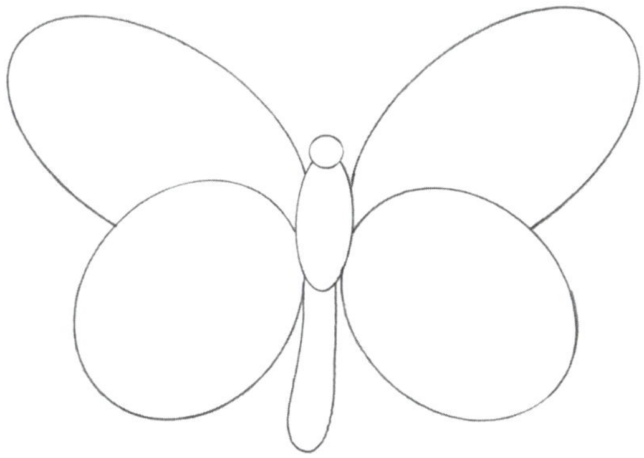

3

4

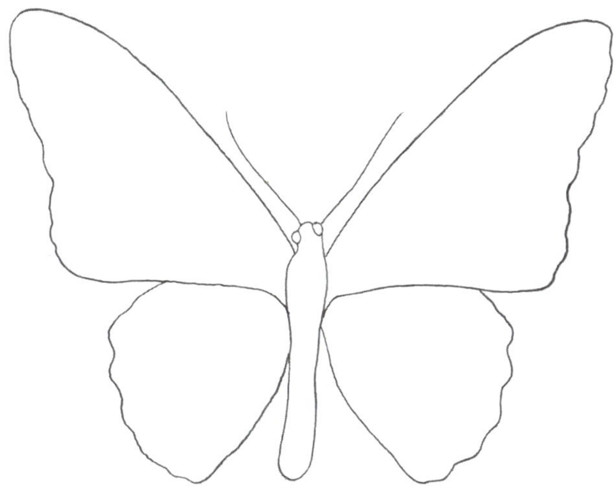

5

6

Grey Crowned Crane

Details

Size: 3 feet long
Diet: Fish, reptiles, insects, amphibians, seeds, and grass
Location: Africa

Did You Know?

The grey crowned crane prefers a wet environment, such as marshes and flood plains, where it can feed on a diverse array of small animals. However, this bird is sometimes spotted in the drier African savannah.

This large, gray bird is known for the crown of golden feathers atop its head. It has red markings on its cheeks and throat, along with a pair of pale blue eyes.

Fun Fact!

The grey crowned crane has an impressive wingspan of 6.5 feet!

1

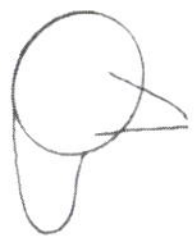

2

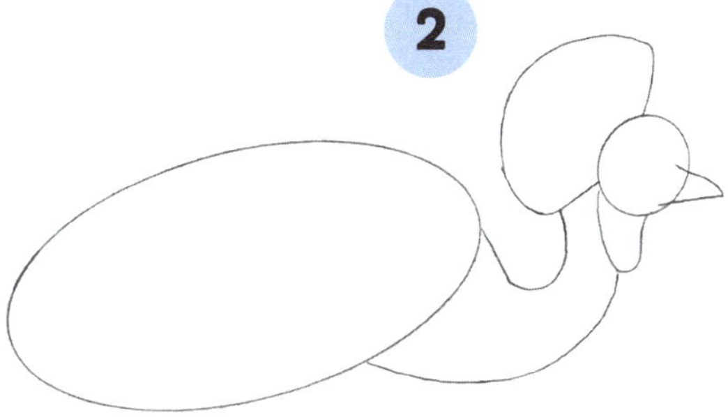

3

4

5

6

Mini Quiz Answers

Page 13: C. On average, it takes about 5 weeks for an egg to hatch and grow into a butterfly.

Page 19: True. Like many other butterfly species, male purple-spotted swallowtails are noticeably brighter in color than females. They are also more aggressive and easier to spot.

Page 21: D. Toronto.

Page 23: B. The Adonis blue female is brown in color.

Page 27: A. The red-banded hairstreak caterpillar loves eating the leaves of a sumac tree.

Page 29: B. Baseball.

Page 33: D. The cedar waxwing primarily eats berries.

Page 41: A. Molting (or moulting) is the process of shedding feathers, which helps the birds replace damaged feathers with new ones.

Page 43: C. The redspot sawtooth is known for its fast flight.

Page 47: B. Large orange tip females are white.

Page 49: False. The kingfisher makes its nest in burrows along the edge of water.

Page 55: D. The ladder-backed woodpecker is not found in Florida.

Page 57: True. The black-veined white butterfly became extinct in Britain during the 1920s.